Mr. Putter and Tabby Walk the Dog

CYNTHIA RYLANT

Mr. Putter and Tabby Walk the Dog

Illustrated by
ARTHUR HOWARD

Scholastic Inc.
New York Toronto London Auckland Sydney

For Herb and Mary
—C. R.

For Cora and Bernie
—A. H.

ISBN 0-590-25959-8

Published by Scholastic Inc., 555 Broadway, New York, NY 10012, by arrangement with Harcourt Brace & Company.

12 11 10 9 8 9/9 0/0

Printed in the U.S.A. 23

First Scholastic printing, April 1995

SPORTS SUNDAY

PLANT FOOD

1

The Lollypup

Mr. Putter and his fine cat, Tabby,
lived next door to
Mrs. Teaberry and her small dog, Zeke.

Mrs. Teaberry sometimes gave
Mr. Putter eggplant for his supper.
And Mr. Putter sometimes gave
Mrs. Teaberry kiwis for her lunch.

They were very happy
living side by side.

One day Mrs. Teaberry slipped
on a kiwi and hurt her foot.
Mr. Putter and Tabby took her
to the doctor.

The doctor said, "This foot needs a rest.
No walking Zeke for a week."
"No walking Zeke for a week?"
cried Mrs. Teaberry.

"But who will walk my little lollypup?"
(She always called Zeke her little lollypup.)

Then Mr. Putter, who had a
very soft heart, said, "I will.
I will walk your little lollypup."
Mrs. Teaberry was happy.

But she was a little worried.

"I hope he doesn't tug," she said.

"Oh, no," said Mr. Putter.

"Zeke won't tug."

"I hope he doesn't wrap around trees,"

she said.

"Oh, no," said Mr. Putter again.

"Zeke won't wrap."

"And I hope he doesn't chase other dogs," she said finally. "Especially the big ones."

"Oh, no," said Mr. Putter for the last time. "Zeke is a good dog."

“Zeke is a fine dog.”

Mr. Putter looked at the little lollypup.

“Zeke is a *dream* dog,” Mr. Putter said

with a smile.

2

The Nightmare

Zeke was a *nightmare*.
The first day Mr. Putter and Tabby
took him for a walk, he tugged.
He tugged and tugged and tugged.

He tugged Mr. Putter and Tabby

through yards

and creeks

and houses
they had never been through before.

When Mr. Putter and Tabby got home,
they had to have some warm milk
and pudding
and a nap.

“Zeke is not a dream dog,”
Mr. Putter said to Tabby
when they woke up.
“Zeke is a nightmare.”

The second day they
took him for a walk,
Zeke wrapped around trees.
He wrapped around
an elm tree.

He wrapped
around a pine tree.

He wrapped
around a pear tree.

And he always wrapped

Mr. Putter and Tabby with him.

When Mr. Putter and Tabby got home,
they had to have some warm milk
and popovers
and a nap.

"Zeke is not a dream dog,"
Mr. Putter said to Tabby
when they woke up.
"Zeke is a nightmare."

The third day Zeke chased dogs.
And he didn't chase little ones.
He chased big ones.

He chased a Russian Wolfhound.

He chased a Great Dane.

He chased a Saint Bernard.

He chased them until they got bored with being chased.

Then they turned around and chased Zeke.

And Mr. Putter.

And Tabby.

The big dogs chased them

through yards

and creeks

and houses

they had never been through before.

When Mr. Putter and Tabby got home,
they had to have some warm milk
and shortbread
and a nap.
“Zeke is not a dream dog,”
Mr. Putter said to Tabby
when they woke up.
“Zeke is a nightmare.”

And the two of them
sat a long time
wondering what to do.
They weren't sure they
could live through
four more days with
the lollypup.

3

The Dream Dog

"Here's the deal, Zeke,"

Mr. Putter said on the fourth day.

"You be a good dog,
and every day after our walk
you'll get a nice surprise."

Zeke was a smart dog.

He knew what a deal was.

The fourth day
he didn't tug,
he didn't wrap,
and he didn't chase.
He was a dream dog.

So Mr. Putter and Tabby took him
to the Frosty Freeze.
Zeke had a hot fudge sundae
with extra cherries.

The fifth day
Zeke didn't tug,
and he didn't wrap,
and he didn't chase.
He was a dream dog again.

So Mr. Putter and Tabby
took him to the swimming pool.
He jumped off the diving board
fifteen times.

On the sixth day

Zeke was a dream dog,

and he went to the carnival.

On the seventh day
Zeke was a dream dog,
and he went to the zoo.

When Mr. Putter and Tabby
took Zeke home for the
last time, Mrs. Teaberry asked,
"Was Zeke a good lollypup?"

And Mr. Putter
(who had brought her pecans
instead of kiwis)
smiled the biggest smile.
He said, “Zeke was a dream lollypup.”

Then he and Tabby said good-bye
and went home
and had a party.

FROSTY